Lollypop Kid

Miranda Maynard

This edition first published in paperback by
Michael Terence Publishing in 2023
www.mtp.agency

Copyright © 2023 Miranda Maynard

Miranda Maynard has asserted the right to be identified as
the author of this work in accordance with the
Copyright, Designs and Patents Act 1988

ISBN 9781800945104

No part of this publication may be reproduced, stored
in a retrieval system, or transmitted, in any form or
by any means, electronic, mechanical, photocopying,
recording or otherwise, without the prior
permission of the publisher

Cover image
Copyright © Obvelov
www.123rf.com

Cover design
Copyright © 2023 Michael Terence Publishing

Michael Terence
Publishing

*With things remembered
the sweet kid's memories still live on…*

Contents

Introduction 1

1: Paper Round Boy 2
2: Bubble Gum Kid 5
3: Children's Tea Party 7
4: The Games the Children Once Played
   at Primary School 10
5: Alone at the Weekend 13
6: The Sweet Kids 14
7: The School Assembly 16
8: Chocolates, Sweets and Schooldays 18
9: Another Hard School-day 20
10: Candy (Lollypop) Kid 21
11: A Fearful Night 22
12: Brothers and Sister Together 23
13: The Birthday Party 25

14: Sweet Tooth 26

15: The Sweet Kid 27

16: Sam (The Lollypop Kid) Gave Sweets to Bullies 29

17: Easter and Christmas (Seasonal Treats) 30

18: A Sweet Delight 32

19: The Grammar School Days 33

20: The Period Before Lunchtime 34

21: The Joyful Pleasure of Sweets 35

22: Grandma's Affectionate Love 37

23: The Teenager's Obsessive (Sweet) Habit 39

24: Sam's Sweet Reflection of Chocolates.
    Sam's First Memories 40

25: Sam's Big Comic Collection 41

Also by Miranda Maynard 45

Introduction

Sam went to a beautiful Infant school. It was officially institutional. Neither of his parents conformed to the dress code.

Sam got attached to his school. Realising his time there would be over. He liked his school.

Subsequently, things changed. An upheaval! When Sam's parents moved house and area.

At the start of the new Autumn Term, Sam started his new C.E. Primary school.

1
Paper Round Boy

Sam did his weekly paper round for the week. At the sweet shop, he gave it up. Instead, he became a Newspaper boy who delivered Newspapers to homes. To those with a subscription.

With his money, Sam bought sweets at a sweet shop Chewing gum, Bubble gum, liquorice and lollypops. His favourite was blackcurrant lollypops.

At home alone in his bedroom, he sat in a corner in his armchair. Sam licked his blackcurrant lollypop. It tasted of a fruity flavour. His mouth was covered in it. Sam usually did not share his sweets with anyone. Not even his Brothers and Sister. (His spiteful Brothers and Sister demanded that he should share his sweets with them. They all insisted on their Brother sharing his sweets.)

Sam had a sweet tooth. He was a candy and lollypop kid. Due to being selfish, Sam did not share his sweets with any of his Brothers and Sister. There were times when they asked him for sweets. Every time Sam refused to give them any.

Sam would pull out both pockets of his trousers. He would say to them calmly, in a soft tone of voice,

"I don't have any."

His Brothers and Sister resented their Brother. They called him selfish.

Alone in his bedroom, sitting in an armchair, Sam ate his sweets to his heart's content. Nothing else gave him such pleasure and enjoyment. It was such a fine pleasurable feeling. Sam loved sweets. He liked lollypops. (The kids at school called him the Lollypop Kid.)

He still did not share any of his sweets with any of them. Sam had an obsession with confectionery. He would meet other school kids buying sweets. The kids liked sweets. It was a childish obsession of theirs. Anything sweet was a favourite of theirs.

Some of them, the selfish ones, did not share their sweets with anyone. Others were generous. They shared their sweets with their friends.

Later in the evening, Sam's Brothers brought their friends home. At a lounge table, they all played Dungeons and Dragons, a board game, under the shining chandelier lights.

Meanwhile, Sam stayed in his large bedroom. Remaining unsociable with regards to everyone else.

Sam staved off his hunger by eating more sweets out of a paper bag. Which he bought at a confectionery shop. He liked sweets. These sweets were an obsession of his. He had uncontrolled urges for it. Sam possessed an obsessiveness for it. He fancied some sweets. A delightful fancy!

Sam envied how his two Brothers and Sister had really good friends. Both his parents remained possessive of their only Daughter.

With defiant refusal, Sam gave none of his nice sweets to any of his Brothers and Sister. With a careless attitude, he remained selfish towards them again and again.

With his fuming Mother in a mood, a temper. Not cooking. All of the children ate a pizza, a takeaway.

Relaxing alone in his bedroom, Sam ate the rest of his favourite sweets. He took some pleasure in eating his sweets. Licking a lollypop. A sweet blackcurrant-flavoured lollypop. His mouth was covered with a mouthful of the runny and sticky lollypop. He in his relaxed and restful state just loved the aftertaste.

2
Bubble Gum Kid

At break time, Sam impressed his friends by showing his big collection of bubble gum film stickers. Meanwhile, a few others swapped their stickers for other ones. They envied how Sam collected stickers. His collection of stickers was thick. The film stickers themselves were a still from a Motion Picture. A film tie-in.

At the next lesson, Sam attended his next class. This Primary School teacher teaching was a hag. Sam dreaded being taught by Mrs Bronx. Mrs Bronx was Germanic, tall, slender and monstrous with small beady eyes.

During the short lesson, Sam read a children's book with the other Primary schoolchildren in a warm classroom which was spick and span.

Sam disliked Mrs Bronx. Mrs Bronx objected to teaching Sam. Mrs Bronx disliked it.

Today Sam left Primary school earlier than usual. Today was a shorter day. Sam got back home. Alone in his bedroom. He turned over the pages of a supplement. There he stuck down the rest of his football stickers in the remaining spaces. He kept his stickers; doubles just in case he might have to swap any of them in the future.

Sam chewed his chewy bubble gum.

The next day after Primary school, Sam saw Mr Stacks. All the groups of schoolchildren queued up at a counter to buy sweets for themselves.

For the shopkeeper using a till it was a busy day. His wife was a cashier.

3
Children's Tea Party

Mrs Dorset dropped off her son, Sam, at Mrs Mariot's house where her son Charlie had invited friends to a tea party at his house.

A small number of children gathered together for a get-together. A nice tea party, organised by Mrs Dorset.

Arriving at Charlie's house, Sam entered the Dining Room. At the Dining table, all of the seats were taken except for one. Sam sat at the far corner of the Dining table. There the dining table was laid with a plain white tablecloth with plastic cutlery, paper cups and paper plates.

All of the hungry children ate a piece of log cake, cheese and cucumber sandwiches and for dessert jelly and soft pieces of peaches. They drank diluted orange squash.

Sam enjoyed his treat. For he appreciated his invitation. His invitation to a tea party. Sam felt pleased. He remained under an obligation. Everyone else he knew quite well. There in the presence of boys sitting at the Dining table, there wasn't even a stranger present. They were good friends of Charlie. Sam remained silent. Everybody else sitting at the Dining table talked. Sam thought it was bad manners to talk when eating at the Dining table in the company of guests.

Charlie had a passion for football. His interest in the sport was obsessional. He rambled on about football. His favourite football club, a team in the League which he supported as a Fan!

As regards Sam, Sam disliked football. He was apathetic about the sport. Even watching it on television actually made him uninterested and unexcited. Watching it remained an utter bore. A televised match or football highlights.

Sam's interest remained his obsessive love for music. He liked to listen to music generally. All sorts of music. Charlie's few friends did not talk about music at all. One of them has an obsession with music as he was a Fan!

He remained coy and reticent about it. As usual, he loved pop music. Another one had a liking for classical music. A student.

Sam enjoyed being present at the tea party. The treat made such a change. It made such a difference. He liked it. It was so good being together again after so long. It was such a good feeling!

Afterwards, everybody getting up had been politely excused to leave at once after sitting at the Dining table. They all stayed longer together. Therefore enjoying everybody else's company. It was a fairly good friendship regarding everybody. A few individuals stayed behind and talked while others left in a hurry to get home. The ones that did stay longer were individuals who were friendly, cool, laidback and easy-going.

Staying longer at Charlie's house. Sam just loved this cosy house. All of the luxurious rooms had luxury and comfort. The interior, décor, furniture, framed pictures and paintings and antiques. As well as taxidermy and exotica. The plush luxury deep pile carpet. Also, the general luxuries of it and comforts.

Sam stayed about an hour at Charlie's before eventually leaving to get home. His Mother picked up her son. An organised arrangement. His Mother was a Chartered Accountant. A professional. A timekeeper and bookkeeper.

4
The Games the Children Once Played at Primary School

The first game Sam played was a game of conkers. A hard conker attached to a long piece of strong string. Sam beat a few others at conkers. At that time, it was a boy's craze playing conkers. His big conker remained intact. This conker he played with was strong and rock-hard. His conker smashed theirs. Their struck conker smashed up.

At another time Sam played another game. This time marbles in the school playground and down on the drains. Sam had a big string bag of marbles. All of the beautiful colourful ones and the ordinary marbles. He gave up playing marbles when he lost many marbles games and when his plenty of marbles were pinched by his elder Brother. His craze for marbles was now over. (At that time there was a shortage of supply at chains for new marbles. None available in stock.)

One day Sam played British Bulldog. The object of this silly game was to run from one end of the playground to the other side. They had to catch persons running from one end to the other end of the playground.

This particular game was rough, brutish and childish. It required brute strength. In the school playground, British Bulldog ended as soon as another game started. There were boys playing football in the playground.

One afternoon an older boy kicked a football in Sam's face accidentally. A rough kid. His hard shot struck Sam's face. It stunned him. Sam was dazed. His face stung. His cheeks flushed. From his injury sustained, Sam stopped playing football in the playground. Recovering from injury. Sam ended up playing bench ball during games.

Months and months later Sam eventually played for the school football team only once. (Sam being accident-prone did not prevent him from playing football.) He was an amateur. He was still amateurish at playing football.

That warm sunny afternoon he played interscholastic with another Primary school on a playing field. A football pitch. Sam's team lost 2-0. During the second half of the game, Sam's shot struck the goalpost. His team failed to score.

Sam ended up being dropped by the school. He lost interest in playing football. Growing older at Primary school, Sam developed a new skill at playing chess. He belonged to the chess club.

He played chess with the chess team at interscholastic. Playing chess at different venues at

Primary schools. Sam ended up playing three chess games. He won one game and lost two games. His school chess team was thrashed.

Unfortunately, Sam was dropped by the school team. At Primary school, the chess club eventually became abolished. Sam still kept playing chess at home. Despite being demoralised and disenchanted.

One day Sam received a new pocket testament. But at that time, it did not really mean anything. Sam was unchristian. An unbeliever. Sam had no faith. He still remained a non-believer. He could not demystify the mysteries of Christianity yet. He was still far too immature to understand the scriptures and Christianity. What was the purpose of being a Christian?

Growing up, everything made him confused, perplexed and baffled at school, in society, and his life. He misunderstood. Not fully understanding anything whatsoever. What was the objective of Christianity? What was the purpose of the scriptures?

At a Primary school or Infant school whichever. One Christmas at an assembly. The school held a Nativity. Sam played a king who knelt down amongst the wise men. This may have been bizarre, and strange at first. But it ended up being spiritually symbolic. An uncanny significance. An actual living testament to one's life!

5
Alone at the Weekend

Sam alone in his bedroom thought of his Primary school friends. How they invited him back to their house. (Two of them both Brothers took Sam back to their house. They both unwelcomed and uninvited Sam in.)

One of them showed Sam his big collection of football stickers and his football team's merchandise.

Another one had a kick-around in the garden at his acquaintance's house in the same road where he once lived. Another so-called friend showed him into his semi-detached house. Sam spent only a short time at his so-called friend's house.

Leaving Primary school. Sam never saw any of them ever again! What did happen to them? They may have been strange and mysterious!

There was a connection but Sam could not figure it out. Sam was too common and naïve. The thing was a coincidence. A coincidental strangeness.

As he grew older, he tried to demystify it. He still could not work it out. He was too small to really understand. The wishful thinker was lost in a daydreamy trance! A reverie. As he engaged in a daydream.

6
The Sweet Kids

During lunchtime, Sam stayed in the school playground. Today he did not go home to get his lunch. Instead, the sweet kid ate his sweets. Coming towards him the other few sweet kids joined Sam in eating their sweets. They enjoyed their sweet time together. The children's sweetness a niceness.

After lunchtime ended. The children attended Registration. They were punctual for their attendance of registration.

Then afterwards all of the children attended their class. There Sam tore open a packet of sweets. Sam chewed soft-centred sweets during class. The flavour of these chewy sweets had various flavours.

Sam got more pleasure from eating his sweets than from doing anything else. He unlistened to the Primary school Teacher speaking to the class. The Teacher was engrossed in teaching.

Sam took pleasure from sucking his sweets Raspberry, blackcurrant, lime and strawberry-flavoured sweets.

As the class were doing their classwork Sam spent his time daydreaming. With his elbow on a table. He leaned his chin on his palm. The dreamy daydreamer looking out of the window at a sideward angle at a corner of a table. Sam daydreamed.

7
The School Assembly

Early in the morning, the children attended the school Assembly. The schoolchildren sat down uncomfortably on a hall wooden floor. It was shiny and polished. Standing they sang hymns from a hymn book. The Headmistress addressed the Primary school. Those Primary schoolchildren were listening with interest.

Straight afterwards Sam attended his Maths class. He did multiplication, subtraction, adding, division and fractions. The ones who got top marks gained a red sticker indicating top marks obtained on a chart. The other stickers in different colours indicated lower marks obtained. There was a sense of competitiveness amongst the bright schoolchildren. One of them was brainy indeed. A clever one.

In the next class, Sam did English. He spent his time reading a book of his choice during the lesson. Presently there were a certain number of children's books to choose from. A limited selection of books from a pile of books on top of a table. He found it hard to choose one. He remained undecided about whichever book to select. He ended up choosing an uncanny one. With a lack of understanding and ignorance. Sam was unaware of what he had been reading. Could this have made him corrupt? Sam enjoyed reading a children's book. A ghost story. He acquired reading and writing skills. A listener and talker. Showing some communicative skills.

On another day the swimming group boarded a coach. They were driven to the swimming baths. Sam disliked swimming. Against his will, he objected to it. Sam ended up swimming with the swimming group for only a few weeks. Learning basic swimming strokes. The dirty coach took the whole swimming group back to their Primary school. In a lovely classroom, they ate a packet of crisps and drank a pint of fresh pasteurized milk from a milk crate. They rested while recovering from fatigue.

During the Christmas season, the Primary school children indulged in their Christmas treat. It was a seasonal enchantment in a lovely warm classroom in dim light. The dark classroom was partially shadowy. It was enchanting from the shining light glowing.

On other days the school children enjoyed having sweets at breaktime and lunchtime. (Sam would usually go home for lunch.)

Sam took delight in eating his sweets as well as everyone else eating their sweets. The sweet kid took great pleasure in it.

Footnote

Sam heard a rumour spread. That the beloved Headmistress had died!
    What was it, a rumour?
    And another one…

8
Chocolates, Sweets and Schooldays

Sam felt depressed today at grammar school. A schoolgirl with crushingly good looks whom the pupil fancied and desired. The schoolboy was attracted to the appealing schoolgirl's sex appeal. The schoolgirl undesired him. He unappealed to her. The schoolboy had a crush on her.

Making him feel depressed and miserable. Sam spent his time alone in his bedroom. He reflected on Jenny with a desire infatuated with Jenny. To overcome his depression and deep misery he fancied some sweets. Satisfying his appetite for sweets.

Also his sister Katie had empathy too in the same way as her Brother who obsessed with his sweets in a paper bag. Katie ate her sweets with her Brother. Katie was unselfish in sharing her sweets with her Brother. Katie a chocoholic indulged in eating luxury milk chocolate nutty and almond ones from out of a tin of chocolates. They were all beautifully wrapped up in some sort of Christmassy wrappings. The beautiful ones.

Eating chocolates did some wonder to Sam. It just made him feel so much better. It enabled Sam to get some comfort at least. A sense of comfort.

Nothing else gave Sam so much comfort.

Sam's schooldays were dreadfully unhappy and miserable. The schoolboy suffered from deep miseries and bouts of depression. He resorted to eating his favourite lollypops, sweets, bags of crisps and bars of chocolate throughout those school years.

9
Another Hard School-day

Leaving school. Crossing over the road. From there he went down the very long narrow path. There he passed by a green playing field.

From there the schoolboy walked down the long road. There he turned left to a street. From a Baker, he bought two cakes and in a sweet shop he bought plenty of sweets and packets of crisp in his favourite crisp flavour.

Coming home Sam relaxed in his armchair in his bedroom. Sam eating up his crisps and sweets. He got such a fine pleasure in eating up his cakes and sweets. Nothing else could really compare to it at all. He felt such great pleasure. The Lollypop Kid took more satisfying pleasure in eating up his fresh cakes from a Baker.

The Gourmand indulged in eating up his cakes and sweets and drinking up canned drinks. He burped, belched and felt bloated. Sam's pleasurable pleasure of eating and drinking was most satisfying. He empathised with gluttony. Sam had some empathy for gluttons. Sam overate. However, he did not quite get to the stage of gluttony, though he did engage in gourmandism quite naturally.

10
Candy (Lollypop) Kid

On one schoolday. Getting back home from grammar school. Sam liked to eat his candy sticks. He preferred this sweet now more than anything else. (Of course, Sam still loved his Lollypops.)

For Sam eating candy remained a pleasurable thing. It was something obsessed. A sweet which was a favourite. A possession obsessiveness! A sweet obsession of his. The assortment of plenty of sweets. He savoured the taste of sweet candy.

Indulging in eating sweets remained pleasurable and the time taken in satisfying his appetite. It was gratifying and enjoyable.

Sam grew up to love candy. He was obsessed with candy. The taste of a sweet flavour of candy made him take delight in it. With ecstatic wonder, he did in fact relish it. He looked forward to buying more sweets tomorrow. Perhaps a lollypop!

11
A Fearful Night

One night Sam could not sleep. He got up and came out of his bedroom. Going out to the landing there he met his angry and violent Father. His Father raised his voice in anger.

"Aren't you asleep? Go to bed. I don't want you to watch television. I will give you a hiding if you do," shouted Father.

Sam was afraid of his Father. Sam went back to his bedroom. He stayed there. He waited in there until his Father went back downstairs.

Meanwhile, Sam sneaked into an upstairs room. It was dark and spacious. On the carpet in the corner, there was a portable black and white television. He switched on the television. A few days ago, he saw Drac Pack. Now he wanted to watch the real one. A Dracula film. Seemingly Sam was frightened that his Father might catch him watching a horror film on television. Sam was fearful of his Father. He heard floorboards creak and sounds of eerie noises. It was a full moon tonight. Sam trembled with fear. Sam sneaked out of a dark room. He came back to his small bedroom. He went back to bed.

Then months and months later his Father abandoned and deserted his son!

12
Brothers and Sister Together

Sam's Brothers and sister sat at the Dining table. They appeared to be cheerful, good-natured and in a happy mood.

From every paper bag, they each emptied sweets onto the Dining table. There on top of the table was an assortment of sweets. They each indulged in eating sweets. This time everyone shared their sweets.

"You have heard about the Samaritan?" said Brother.

"Oh! Yes. What's that got to do with it?" questioned Sam.

"Let bygones be bygones," insisted Sister.

At present hardly talking anymore to anyone, they all took delight in eating their sweets. Nothing else gave them such fine pleasure. They indulged in eating their favourite sweets. (Katie an obsessive chocoholic ate the chocolatey ones.)

Today that pleasant afternoon the two Brothers and Sister were so pleased and happy together. They took great pleasure in being together. At eating such fine sweets.

Tomorrow Sam intended to go to the confectionery as it was an obsessional intention of his. At the confectionery, he intended to spend his money on his favourite sweets.

For Sam, an assortment of confection was tempting, an obsessive irresistibleness.

Going to a confectionery he felt like a kid in a candy store. There he met townspeople and town kids. With a childish obsession, they empathised. They had empathy. Sam bought plenty of sweets. He liked his choice of confection. He was satisfied with what sweets he had bought at the confectionery. He had been self-indulgent.

On another day Sam ate all his sweets. Both his Brothers and Sister had no more sweets either. So he settled on eating a packet of biscuits to satisfy his appetite. He ate wholemeal biscuits.

Whilst everyone prepared themselves for the start of the New Term at their new school. Sam spent his time eating up his sweets. In preparation for the confection, he prepared himself to buy his favourites – sweets.

13
The Birthday Party

Going to Ricky's Birthday party at his house. There he gave his friend a birthday present. Ricky approved of his friend's present. Ricky rather liked it. A toy car.

Ricky favoured his friend. With approval, Ricky admired his shiny new toy car.

Sitting at the Dining table, Ricky Stam made a wish!

Ricky blew out all of the candles on a Birthday cake. Mrs Stam, Ricky's Mother, holding a sharp kitchen knife sliced the thick chocolate cake evenly. Giving everybody a slice of cake each on a new paper plate. Everybody liked their piece of cake. A gâteau with chocolatey flake.

Sam only stayed a short time at Ricky's Birthday party. Ricky's parents were well off.

Within half an hour, Sam's Mother came to pick up her son and take him home. As Sam got back home, he hurried out of the car. Quickly he entered the house. Going upstairs to his bedroom. He ate the rest of his sweets. He licked a blackcurrant lollypop with a fruity flavour. How he liked it!

The Lollypop Kid rounded off his day by eating a lollypop. There he relaxed in the armchair in a position of nice comfort. He enjoyed listening to music.

14
Sweet Tooth

Sam had another hard day at Grammar School. He indeed failed his Tests. (Ultimately, he knew he would probably fail all of his Examinations, it was imminent.)

Failing was something of a tendency, a common thing.

Other pupils tended to do much better than he did. He envied the clever pupils. The schoolgirls snubbed and shunned the lonely schoolboy who was a loner.

For Sam eating sweets was a childish obsession. A thing he was rather obsessed with in his teens. Meeting other pupils who had the same thing in common, a pleasant sweetness!

When Sam got back home, he stayed in his bedroom. He sat down in an armchair. He unwound as he rested. He ate his leftover bags of sweets.

The sweet tooth thrilled with joy at eating up the rest of his sweets which also included a blackcurrant lollypop which he chewed up. Swallowing it up in mouthfuls.

15
The Sweet Kid

At primary school, the sweet kid ate his favourite sweets. That school day at lunchtime Sam did not pay attention to anyone else in the playground. His intentions were to eat his nice sweets. He took some comfort in eating his sweets. His obsessional favourites.

He did not share his sweets with anyone. A few other schoolkids bought sweets from a local sweet shop down the street.

At home alone with his Brothers and Sister. Sam took sweet delight in eating his sweets with both Brothers and Sister which he thoughtfully shared with them. They had a pleasant time together with brotherly love towards his Brothers and being nice towards his sweet Sister made the difference.

Both Brothers and Sister treated Sam their Brother to a fair share of their sweets which was a delightful favourite of theirs. They loved their sweets. Also the sweet kid too. They all ate their sweets. They threw away all their sweet wrappings in a waste paper bin. Sam felt aphrodisiac having eaten the chocolatey flavoured ones. He ate chocolates too which Katie his Sister gave him. With an obligational inclination to treat their Brother.

By showing her Brother with a motivational intention and an inclinational favour towards him.

16
Sam (The Lollypop Kid) Gave Sweets to Bullies

On one Thursday afternoon at Grammar school in the playground. A few Bullies surrounded Sam somewhere in the playground. Forcing him backwards in a direction anywhere. Sam was afraid of them. He was scared of being beaten up. He felt fearful again.

He thought of an idea. A survival one!

He took his bag of sweets out of his blazer pocket. He offered them sweets. From his own form, the Bullies saw Sam holding a paper bag of sweets.

Unappreciating the thoughtful member of Form. They each took a handful of sweets out of a paper bag. Sam stuffed the bag of sweets in his blazer pocket.

Sam slipped away from them, losing them amidst the crowds of schoolchildren. The schoolboy was relieved to get away. The paper bag of sweets he possessed had saved him from being bullied again by a few Bullies from his own Form. The sweet kid had survived again from bullying.

After lunchtime had ended Sam attended Form Registration. The pupil was attending the final periods of his school-day.

17
Easter and Christmas (Seasonal Treats)

During Easter time Sam ate a piece of milk chocolate from a luxury Easter Egg and also a few fruity chewy sweets in a packet inside an Easter Egg.

The Easter Egg had been shared by his family.

Sam liked the Easter treat as it was an Easter (season) tradition.

Sometimes at Easter, his sister Katie treated herself to an Easter Egg. A typical Easter tradition.

Katie loved chocolate.

At Christmastime Sam and his Brothers and Sister enjoyed the seasonal Christmas treat of eating up chocolates and chewy sweets which were in a Christmas stocking.

At Christmas, the family fancied an assortment of sweets and chocolates at the festivity. They all indulged in eating it up to their joyful hearts' content.

They took comfort from luxuries and the pleasure of Christmas itself.

(At Easter they all relished their treat of eating up a whole Easter Egg shared amongst their family. It was one of their most favourite treats!)

18
A Sweet Delight

One day Sam spent time with both of his Brothers and Sister. They offered to share a fair amount of their sweets with their Brother.

Sam deeply appreciated his Brothers' and Sister's generosities. Showing brotherly and sisterly kindness to their appreciative Brother.

From his Brothers and Sister Sam took more and more sweets. They were generous, unselfish and thoughtful.

Enjoying the (cherished) moment. He was greatly delighted. Sam had plenty of sweets and it made Sam feel so much happier! It was a sweet bliss! Sam was an excited and overjoyed candy kid! He experienced something of a childish joy. Sam took great pleasure in it. He cherished the moment of being alone together with his Brothers and Sister. Sam had a blissful time with them. His Brothers and Sister took the opportunity to make up to their Brother. Giving their Brother sweets galore. As a forgiven token, a reconciliation of their love! In reconciliation.

19
The Grammar School Days

In summer today at Grammar school in the playground. None of the pupils there gave Sam any sweets. So, Sam avoided them. The schoolboy took purposeful measures. The pupil had disrespect and disregard for the mean and selfish ones and humiliators. Some of those schoolboys and schoolgirls were condescending and patronising.

Sam stayed in a corner of the playground. There he stood still and ate his sweets without being intruded on by others. With a peaceful nature, he enjoyed his peace. Standing in a shadow. His indulgence was a usual regular pattern of his. He took sweet delight in eating up his sweets. How Sam relished it! (The schoolboy going to a Tuck shop remained an obsessional thing of his. There he queued up and waited to be served. Usually, he bought sweets, bars of chocolate and a can of soft drink.)

20
The Period Before Lunchtime

Before the Geography lesson started, Louise a member of Form asked Sam if he had got any sweets. Sam was attentive to Louise. A Form member. Sam took out a packet of sweets from his sports bag. He stretched out to reach Louise. Sam offered Louise sweets. Sam having feelings had favoured her. Louise took sweets out of a packet.

Louise unappreciated it. By showing no thanks. Louise took it for granted.

Sam who was unthoughtful and selfish did not offer any sweets to anyone else.

During that period Sam took joyful delight in eating a few sweets. He looked forward to lunchtime when he would eat more sweets to satisfy his appetite for sweets.

Today on that particular school day that warm afternoon Sam did not play football in a playground with his schoolfellows. At that time, he wasn't in the mood for playing football. He isolated himself from everybody. Staying alone somewhere out in the school grounds.

21
The Joyful Pleasure of Sweets

Going home from Grammar school. Sam came into his bedroom. He stayed in his bedroom for quite a long time. He sat down in an armchair where he relaxed and rested. He was quite comfortable sitting in a position. Sam took pleasurable comfort at the comfort of being seated. He was humiliated by failure. (He sensed he would fail his Examinations. It was an inevitable failure. With no question of a doubt.)

Sam took the time to eat up his sweets. He had an obsessional love for packets of sweets. Especially fruity flavour ones, candy, liquorice and bars of chocolate.

He took some comfort from eating up his sweets. A joyful comfort it was and a comfort of joy!

Suddenly Katie came into her Brother's bedroom. Katie made an effort to comfort her Brother. The affectionate Sister put her arms around her Brother.

"Eat up your sweets. You mustn't worry. Don't panic. Everything will be alright," said Sister assuredly.

Sam doubted.

"Katie. I hope so. I do hope it will be OK," said Sam doubtfully.

Katie left her Brother alone by himself.

Sam sat alone in his bedroom. Sam was sulky, sullen and moody. He was relieved that it was the weekend. He heaved a sigh of relief.

22
Grandma's Affectionate Love

The Grandson came to see his Grandma. Grandma treated her Grandson with sweets. Sam took wonder at the surprise. He took delight in it. Grandma always treated her Grandson with sweets. Sam loved his Grandma. Grandma made an allowance for her Grandson.

Grandma made tea for her Grandson whenever her Grandson came to see her.

Grandma advised and disciplined her Grandson. Grandma was experienced, mellow and had such wisdom. A spinster!

Sam often listened to his Grandma's words of wisdom.

Today in the afternoon Grandma had treated her Grandson to sweets. The thrilled Grandson appreciated his surprise. He felt deeply appreciative of his Grandma. In her Grandmother's arms, Grandma held her Grandson.

"My Boy!" exclaimed Grandmother joyously.

With deep love, Grandmother rocked her Grandson passionately from side to side. Grandma showed deep affection towards her Grandson. With childish love and affection, he showed to his Grandma. He clung to her affectionately. The Grandson was rocked by his Grandma. Grandma had smothered her Grandson with deep love!

23
The Teenager's Obsessive (Sweet) Habit

Sam possessed an obsessiveness for sweets. It was a habitual obsession of his. He would normally buy sweets and eat them up. He had a "sweet" love, particularly for candy and lollypops.

As a Teenager growing up, nothing else gave him such joy in life. Sam eating up his sweets made him ecstatically happy. (Sam had a confection obsession. A typical possession obsessiveness for it!)

With childish wonder, Sam was excited every time he shopped at confectioneries.

24
Sam's Sweet Reflection of Chocolates.
Sam's First Memories

Going down a road where he once lived when he was small. There he met an elderly stranger giving him a chocolate. The old lady took it out of her handbag. Who is this choc fiend?

Ultimately this led to Sam's eventual liking for chocolates. Sam's Sister had an obsessive love for chocolate. Usually, Katie was obsessed with chocolate.

His unselfish Sister shared her chocolate with her Brother.

Sam approved of his generous Sister. Sam had a liking for Belgian and Swiss chocolate which he munched with a delirious childish delight!

At that present time, nothing else gave Sam such joy and pleasure!

25
Sam's Big Comic Collection

On a hot afternoon in a sun-drenched bedroom. The radiant sunlight shone through the big windows. Sam ate sweets to his heart's content while reading a comic.

Suddenly his Brother burst into his bedroom. Sam had been disturbed by his Brother's intrusion. Sam lost his concentration on reading a comic. Followed by an annual.

"Have you got the first issue?" asked Brother.

Both Sam and his older Brother collected comics. They had a big collection of comics stored in cardboard boxes inside a closet.

Sam looked up. "I might have," said Sam unsurely.

"Well. Find it. Get it out," urged Brother. "We'll be rich!"

The wishful thinker smiled beatifically.

"Yeah. We will. Won't we!"

Sam holding a paper bag of sweets in his hand. Sam offered his Brother some sweets. Sam put a crumpled-up paper bag of sweets on top of the table. Sam licked a lollypop. His favourite flavour.

"This is a good day! We don't have days like this!" sighed Sam.

- THE END -

Also by Miranda Maynard

*Available worldwide from Amazon
and in all good boostores*

Michael Terence Publishing

www.mtp.agency

www.facebook.com/mtp.agency

@mtp_agency

www.ingramcontent.com/pod-product-compliance
Lightning Source LLC
LaVergne TN
LVHW051217070526
838200LV00063B/4945